T0155311

BARTON PEVERIL LIBRARY
1997
SEP. 1997
24. SEP. 1998
20. OCT. 1999
CHECKED
26 NOV 2015
26 MAY 2011
- 9 MAR 2016
Barton Peveril College Library

Music makes pictures and often tells stories, all of it magic and all of it true.

And all of the pictures and all of the stories, and all of the magic, the music is you.

- John Denver-

I Dedicate This Book To Glenn & Muffy And In Loving Memory Of Goppy.
Your Gifts Of Sunshine Warm My Heart And Spirit Everyday.—CC

The publishers wish to thank children's literary agent Sandy Ferguson Fuller of Alp Arts Company, Golden, Colorado, who originally conceived the idea (while John Denver was still alive) of bringing John's spirit to children through picture books, and even after his passing, pursued it to fruition; Hal Thau, John's long-time friend and business manager, who consistently supported the project; Jim Bell of Bell Licensing, Norwalk, Connecticut, and Michael Connelly and Keith Hauprich of Cherry Lane Music Publishing Company, who put it together; the Warner-Chappell Music Company for their support; and BMG Music Company for their courtesy with respect to "The Music Is You."

First Edition
10 9
Book Design by Christopher Canyon Production by Christopher Canyon & Andrea Miles Prepress by Andrea Miles
Copyright © 2003 Dawn Publications / Illustrations copyright © 2003 Christopher Canyon

All rights reserved. No part of this book may be reproduced or transmitted to any form or by any means, electronic or mechanical, including photocopying, recording, or by any information and retrieval system without written permission from the publisher. "Sunshine On My Shoulders" Words & Music by John Denver, Dick Kniss & Mike Taylor, copyright © 1971 Cherry Lane Music Publishing Company, Inc. (ASCAP), DreamWorks Songs (ASCAP), Anna Kate Deutschendorf, Zachary Deutschendorf (administered by Cherry Lane Music Company, Inc.) / Jesse Belle Denver (administered by Warner/Chappell Music). All Rights Reserved. Used By Permission. "The Music Is You" Words & Music by John Denver, copyright © 1974 Cherry Lane Music Publishing Company, Inc. (ASCAP), renewed and assigned to Anna Kate Deutschendorf, Zachary Deutschendorf (administered by Cherry Lane Music Publishing Company, Inc. (ASCAP)) and Jesse Belle Denver (administered by Warner/Chappell Music (ASCAP)). All Rights Reserved. Used By Permission. With respect to "The Music Is You" by John Denver shall mean (P) 1974 RCA Records. Courtesy of BMG Music, under license from BMG Special Products. All Rights Reserved. Used By Permission. Manufactured by Regent Publishing Services, Hong Kong Printed June 2018 in Shenzhen, Guangdong, China

Library of Congress Cataloging-in-Publication Data

Canyon, Christopher.
John Denver's Sunshine on my shoulders / adapted & illustrated by Christopher Canyon.-- 1st ed.
p. cm.
Summary: A picture book adaptation of John Denver's song Sunshine on my shoulders, which celebrates the simple things in life such as sunshine, being in nature, and loving relationships.
ISBN 1-58469-048-8 (hardback with CD) -- ISBN 1-58469-049-6 (hardback)
-- ISBN 1-58469-050-X (pbk.)
1. Children's songs--Texts. [1. Sunshine--Songs and music. 2. Songs.]
I. Title: Sunshine on my shoulders. II. Denver, John. III. Title.
PZ8.3.C1925Jo 2003
782.42--dc21 2003004118

John Denver's

Sunshine On My Shoulders

Adapted & Illustrated by Christopher Canyon

DAWN PUBLICATIONS

Sunshine on my shoulders

makes me happy,

Sunshine in my eyes

can make me cry.

Sunshine on the water
looks so lovely,

Sunshine almost always
makes me high.

If I had a day
that I could give you,

I'd give to you
a day just like today.

If I had a song
that I could sing for you,
I'd sing a song to make you feel this way.

Sunshine on my shoulders
makes me happy,

Sunshine in my eyes can
make me cry.

Sunshine on the water
looks so lovely.

Sunshine almost always
makes me high.

If I had a tale
that I could tell you,

I'd tell a tale
sure to make you smile.

If I had a wish
that I could wish for you,

I'd make a wish
for sunshine all the while.

Sunshine on my shoulders
makes me happy,

Sunshine in my eyes
can make me cry.

Sunshine on the water

looks so lovely,

Sunshine almost always
makes me high,
Sunshine almost

all the time makes me high,
Sunshine almost always...

John Denver knew that the most wonderful things in life are simple and free. Things like sunshine and friendship. He shared his feelings in poetry and song—and with his remarkably expressive voice, millions of people responded. "People everywhere are the same in heart and spirit," he said. "No matter what language we speak, what color we are, the form of our politics or the expression of our love and our faith, music proves it: we are the same." He wrote "Sunshine On My Shoulders" during the difficult times of the Vietnam War. It was a tonic for anxiety, and a reminder of the good, pure things in life. As John said, "when things were seemingly out of control, here was a dove coming back with news of dry land. Or at least a song that soared upward, and took its audience back home." It hit the top of the charts, along with many of his other songs. Over 32 million John Denver albums have sold in the United States alone, making him one of the top selling vocal artists of all time.

Photo courtesy of Lowell Norman

John Denver's son Zak gets a ride.

Yet John Denver was much more than an entertainer. He believed that everyone can make a difference, so he put his feelings into action. He co-founded the Hunger Project, which is committed to ending world hunger forever (www.thp.org). He created Plant-It 2000, now renamed Plant-It 2020, an organization that has already planted one million trees (www.plantit2020.org.). He bought nearly 1000 acres of spectacular Colorado land and gave it to the Windstar Foundation (www.wstar.org) to carry on environmental education. He was a director and supporter of over 22 environmental organizations including the National Wildlife Federation, Save The Children, the Cousteau Society, Friends of the Earth, and the Human/Dolphin Foundation.

Even with all of his charitable activity, he kept writing songs and singing until his death in 1997 when a small experimental plane that he was soloing (John loved to fly!) crashed into the Pacific Ocean. This book and ones to follow, featuring some of his other songs, are dedicated to bringing to children the message of sunshine.

As a child, Christopher Canyon was deeply touched by John Denver. "John's songs gave me hope, joy, and an unbounded belief in possibilities," he says. "'Sunshine On My Shoulders' is a beautiful, moving song of giving, sharing and appreciation. I feel the most powerful aspect of the song is its pure sincerity." Christopher is an award winning artist, musician and performer dedicated to sharing the joy and importance of the arts with children, educators and families. He frequently visits schools, providing entertaining and educational programs and is a popular speaker at conferences throughout the country. "Everyone has what it takes to be artistic, and it's not talent. It is our creativity," he says. "As humans we are all creative beings and our individual creativity is one of our most powerful gifts. If we celebrate and use our creativity it is amazing how much we can learn, how much we can discover and how much joy we have." Christopher also illustrated three other books in the "John Denver & Kids" series: *Take Me Home, Country Roads*; *Grandma's Feather Bed*; and *Ancient Rhymes: A Dolphin Lullaby*. Other titles include *The Tree in the Ancient Forest* and *Stickeen: John Muir and the Brave Little Dog*. He lives in historic German Village in Columbus, Ohio with his artist wife Jeanette Canyon and their three feline children.

Photo courtesy of Jeanette Canyon

Dawn Publications is dedicated to inspiring in children a deeper understanding and appreciation for all life on Earth. Some titles present particular animals, habitats or aspects of nature; others focus on more universal qualities. In each case, our purpose is to encourage a life-long bond with the natural world. To review our titles, please visit us at www.dawnpub.com, or call 800-545-7475.